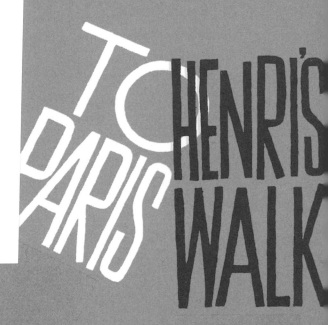

TCHENRI'S
PARIS
WALK

Published in the United States of America in 2012 by Universe Publishing,
a division of Rizzoli International Publications, Inc.
300 Park Avenue South • New York, NY 10010 • www.rizzoliusa.com

First published in 1962 by Young Scott Books

Illustrations © 1962, 2012 Saul Bass
© 2012 Universe Publishing

2012 2013 2014 2015 2016 / 10 9 8 7 6 5 4 3

Printed in Asia

Library of Congress Control Number: 2011934730

ISBN: 978-0-7893-2263-0

ILLUSTRATED BY SAUL BASS • STORY BY LEONORE KLEIN

UNIVERSE

PARIS IS WONDERFUL PARIS IS SPRINGTIME PARIS IS LOVELY PARIS IS BEAUTIFUL PARIS IS FU
SUNSHINE PARIS IS RAINDROPS PARIS IS WONDERFUL PARIS IS SPRINGTIME PARIS IS LOVELY
IS LOVELY PARIS IS BEAUTIFUL PARIS IS FUN PARIS IS MANY PEOPLE PARIS IS COLOR PARIS
PARIS IS WONDERFUL PARIS IS SPRINGTIME PARIS IS LOVELY PARIS IS BEAUTIFUL PARIS IS FU
SUNSHINE PARIS IS RAINDROPS PARIS IS WONDERFUL PARIS IS SPRINGTIME PARIS IS LOVELY
IS LOVELY PARIS IS BEAUTIFUL PARIS IS FUN PARIS IS MANY PEOPLE PARIS IS COLOR PARIS
PARIS IS WONDERFUL PARIS IS SPRINGTIME PARIS IS LOVELY PARIS IS BEAUTIFUL PARIS IS FU
SUNSHINE PARIS IS RAINDROPS PARIS IS WONDERFUL PARIS IS SPRINGTIME PARIS IS LOVELY
IS LOVELY PARIS IS BEAUTIFUL PARIS IS FUN PARIS IS MANY PEOPLE PARIS IS COLOR PARIS
PARIS IS WONDERFUL PARIS IS SPRINGTIME PARIS IS LOVELY PARIS IS BEAUTIFUL PARIS IS FU
SUNSHINE PARIS IS RAINDROPS PARIS IS WONDERFUL PARIS IS SPRINGTIME PARIS IS LOVELY
IS LOVELY PARIS IS BEAUTIFUL PARIS IS FUN PARIS IS MANY PEOPLE PARIS IS COLOR PARIS
PARIS IS WONDERFUL PARIS IS SPRINGTIME PARIS IS LOVELY PARIS IS BEAUTIFUL PARIS IS FU
SUNSHINE PARIS IS RAINDROPS PARIS IS WONDERFUL PARIS IS SPRINGTIME PARIS IS LOVELY
IS LOVELY PARIS IS BEAUTIFUL PARIS IS FUN PARIS IS MANY PEOPLE PARIS IS COLOR PARIS
PARIS IS WONDERFUL PARIS IS SPRINGTIME PARIS IS LOVELY PARIS IS BEAUTIFUL PARIS IS FU
SUNSHINE PARIS IS RAINDROPS PARIS IS WONDERFUL PARIS IS SPRINGTIME PARIS IS LOVELY
IS LOVELY PARIS IS BEAUTIFUL PARIS IS FUN PARIS IS MANY PEOPLE PARIS IS COLOR PARIS
PARIS IS WONDERFUL PARIS IS SPRINGTIME PARIS IS LOVELY PARIS IS BEAUTIFUL PARIS IS FU
SUNSHINE PARIS IS RAINDROPS PARIS IS WONDERFUL PARIS IS SPRINGTIME PARIS IS LOVELY
IS LOVELY PARIS IS BEAUTIFUL PARIS IS FUN PARIS IS MANY PEOPLE PARIS IS COLOR PARIS
PARIS IS WONDERFUL PARIS IS SPRINGTIME PARIS IS LOVELY PARIS IS BEAUTIFUL PARIS IS FU
SUNSHINE PARIS IS RAINDROPS PARIS IS WONDERFU **THIS IS HENRI. HENRI IS READING ABOUT**
IS LOVELY PARIS IS BEAUTIFUL PARIS IS FUN PARIS IS MANY PEOPLE PARIS IS COLOR PARIS
PARIS IS WONDERFUL PARIS IS SPRINGTIME PARIS IS LOVELY PARIS IS BEAUTIFUL PARIS IS FU
SUNSHINE PARIS IS RAINDROPS PARIS IS WONDERFUL PARIS IS SPRINGTIME PARIS IS LOVELY
IS LOVELY PARIS IS BEAUTIFUL PARIS IS FUN PARIS IS MANY PEOPLE PARIS IS COLOR PARIS
PARIS IS WONDERFUL PARIS IS SPRINGTIME PARIS IS LOVELY PARIS IS BEAUTIFUL PARIS IS FU
SUNSHINE PARIS IS RAINDROPS PARIS IS WONDERFUL PARIS IS SPRINGTIME PARIS IS LOVELY
IS LOVELY PARIS IS BEAUTIFUL PARIS IS FUN PARIS IS MANY PEOPLE PARIS IS COLOR PARIS
PARIS IS WONDERFUL PARIS IS SPRINGTIME PARIS IS LOVELY PARIS IS BEAUTIFUL PARIS IS FU
SUNSHINE PARIS IS RAINDROPS PARIS IS WONDERFUL PARIS IS SPRINGTIME PARIS IS LOVELY
IS LOVELY PARIS IS BEAUTIFUL PARIS IS FUN PARIS IS MANY PEOPLE PARIS IS COLOR PARIS
PARIS IS WONDERFUL PARIS IS SPRINGTIME PARIS IS LOVELY PARIS IS BEAUTIFUL PARIS IS FU
SUNSHINE PARIS IS RAINDROPS PARIS IS WONDERFUL PARIS IS SPRINGTIME PARIS IS LOVELY
IS LOVELY PARIS IS BEAUTIFUL PARIS IS FUN PARIS IS MANY PEOPLE PARIS IS COLOR PARIS
PARIS IS WONDERFUL PARIS IS SPRINGTIME PARIS IS LOVELY PARIS IS BEAUTIFUL PARIS IS FU
SUNSHINE PARIS IS RAINDROPS PARIS IS WONDERFUL PARIS IS SPRINGTIME PARIS IS LOVELY
IS LOVELY PARIS IS BEAUTIFUL PARIS IS FUN PARIS IS MANY PEOPLE PARIS IS COLOR PARIS

ARIS IS MANY PEOPLE PARIS IS COLOR PARIS IS WARM PARIS IS A GOOD SMELL PARIS IS A

IS IS BEAUTIFUL PARIS IS FUN PARIS IS MANY PEOPLE PARIS IS COLOR PARIS IS RAINDROPS

WARM PARIS IS A GOOD SMELL PARIS IS SUNSHINE PARIS IS RAINDROPS PARIS IS WONDERFUL

ARIS IS MANY PEOPLE PARIS IS COLOR PARIS IS WARM PARIS IS A GOOD SMELL PARIS IS A

IS IS BEAUTIFUL PARIS IS FUN PARIS IS MANY PEOPLE PARIS IS COLOR PARIS IS RAINDROPS

WARM PARIS IS A GOOD SMELL PARIS IS SUNSHINE PARIS IS RAINDROPS PARIS IS WONDERFUL

ARIS IS MANY PEOPLE PARIS IS COLOR PARIS IS WARM PARIS IS A GOOD SMELL PARIS IS A

IS IS BEAUTIFUL PARIS IS FUN PARIS IS MANY PEOPLE PARIS IS COLOR PARIS IS RAINDROPS

WARM PARIS IS A GOOD SMELL PARIS IS SUNSHINE PARIS IS RAINDROPS PARIS IS WONDERFUL

ARIS IS MANY PEOPLE PARIS IS COLOR PARIS IS WARM PARIS IS A GOOD SMELL PARIS IS A

IS IS BEAUTIFUL PARIS IS FUN PARIS IS MANY PEOPLE PARIS IS COLOR PARIS IS RAINDROPS

WARM PARIS IS A GOOD SMELL PARIS IS SUNSHINE PARIS IS RAINDROPS PARIS IS WONDERFUL

ARIS IS MANY PEOPLE PARIS IS COLOR PARIS IS WARM PARIS IS A GOOD SMELL PARIS IS A

IS IS BEAUTIFUL PARIS IS FUN PARIS IS MANY PEOPLE PARIS IS COLOR PARIS IS RAINDROPS

WARM PARIS IS A GOOD SMELL PARIS IS SUNSHINE PARIS IS RAINDROPS PARIS IS WONDERFUL

ARIS IS MANY PEOPLE PARIS IS COLOR PARIS IS WARM PARIS IS A GOOD SMELL PARIS IS A

PARIS. FUL PARIS IS FUN PARIS IS MANY PEOPLE PARIS IS COLOR PARIS IS RAINDROPS

WARM PARIS IS A GOOD SMELL PARIS IS SUNSHINE PARIS IS RAINDROPS PARIS IS WONDERFUL

ARIS IS MANY PEOPLE PARIS IS COLOR PARIS IS WARM PARIS IS A GOOD SMELL PARIS IS A

IS IS BEAUTIFUL PARIS IS FUN PARIS IS MANY PEOPLE PARIS IS COLOR PARIS IS RAINDROPS

WARM PARIS IS A GOOD SMELL PARIS IS SUNSHINE PARIS IS RAINDROPS PARIS IS WONDERFUL

PARIS IS MANY PEOPLE PARIS IS COLOR PARIS IS WARM PARIS IS A GOOD SMELL PARIS IS A

IS IS BEAUTIFUL PARIS IS FUN PARIS IS MANY PEOPLE PARIS IS COLOR PARIS IS RAINDROPS

WARM PARIS IS A GOOD SMELL PARIS IS SUNSHINE PARIS IS RAINDROPS PARIS IS WONDERFUL

ARIS IS MANY PEOPLE PARIS IS COLOR PARIS IS WARM PARIS IS A GOOD SMELL PARIS IS A

IS IS BEAUTIFUL PARIS IS FUN PARIS IS MANY PEOPLE PARIS IS COLOR PARIS IS RAINDROPS

WARM PARIS IS A GOOD SMELL PARIS IS SUNSHINE PARIS IS RAINDROPS PARIS IS WONDERFUL

ARIS IS MANY PEOPLE PARIS IS COLOR PARIS IS WARM PARIS IS A GOOD SMELL PARIS IS A

IS IS BEAUTIFUL PARIS IS FUN PARIS IS MANY PEOPLE PARIS IS COLOR PARIS IS RAINDROPS

WARM PARIS IS A GOOD SMELL PARIS IS SUNSHINE PARIS IS RAINDROPS PARIS IS WONDERFUL

ARIS IS MANY PEOPLE PARIS IS COLOR PARIS IS WARM PARIS IS A GOOD SMELL PARIS IS A

IS IS BEAUTIFUL PARIS IS FUN PARIS IS MANY PEOPLE PARIS IS COLOR PARIS IS RAINDROPS

WARM PARIS IS A GOOD SMELL PARIS IS SUNSHINE PARIS IS RAINDROPS PARIS IS WONDERFUL

HENRI DOES NOT LIVE IN PARIS, BUT HE WISHES HE DID. HENRI LIVES IN REBOUL. REBOUL IS A LITTLE CITY NEAR PARIS. HENRI LIVES IN A NICE HOUSE WITH FLOWERS AT THE WINDOW AND GOOD SOUP ON THE STOVE. HENRI'S MOTHER AND FATHER ARE VERY GOOD TO HENRI.

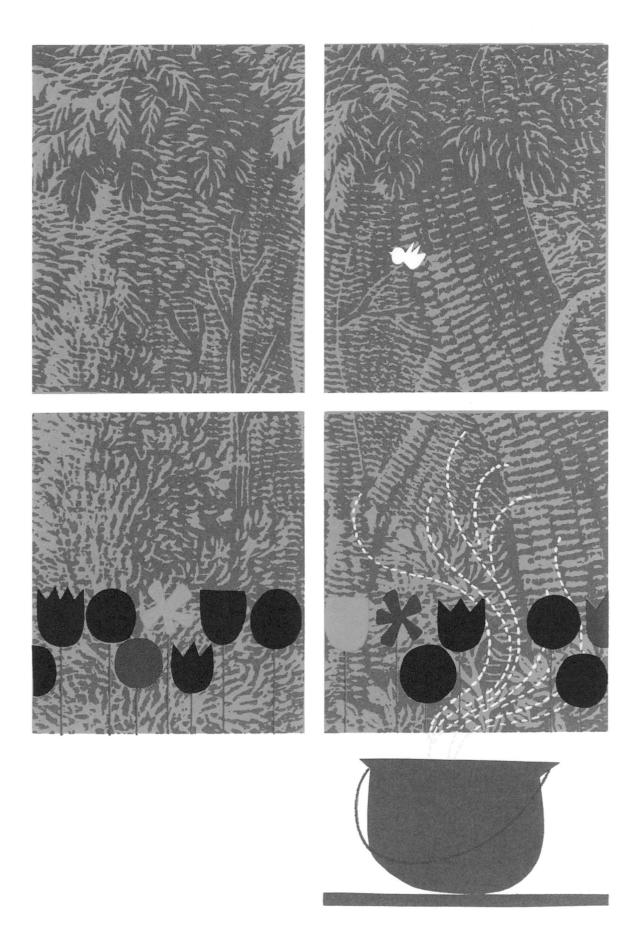

OUTSIDE,
HENRI'S
HOUSE IS
NICE TOO.
IT IS
LITTLE AND
WHITE.

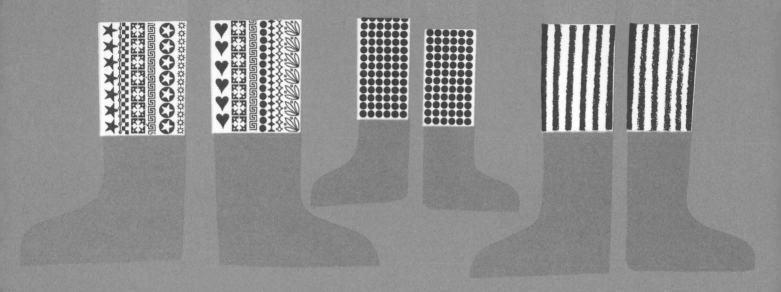

HENRI HAS THREE GOOD FRIENDS, ANDRE, JACQUES AND MICHEL.
HENRI TELLS HIS GOOD FRIENDS MANY THINGS ABOUT PARIS.

"IN PARIS"
SAYS HENRI,
"THERE ARE
THOUSANDS
OF BUSES!!!"

HERE, IN REBOUL, THERE IS ONLY ONE.

HENRI AND HIS FRIENDS LIKE TO PLAY IN THE PARK IN REBOUL. THE PARK HAS
ONLY FIVE TREES, ONE SQUIRREL, AND A LITTLE GRAY CHURCH IN THE MIDDLE.

IN PARIS, HENRI TELLS HIS FRIENDS, THERE ARE MANY BEAUTIFUL CHURCHES.

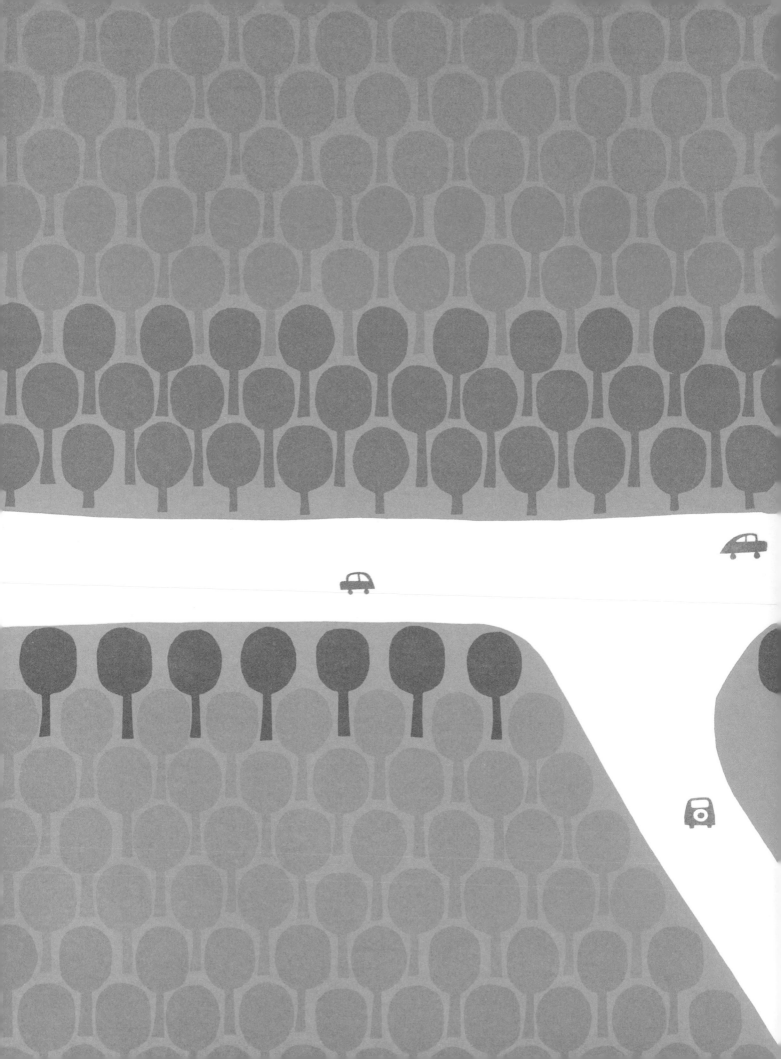

THERE ARE THOUSANDS OF TREES.

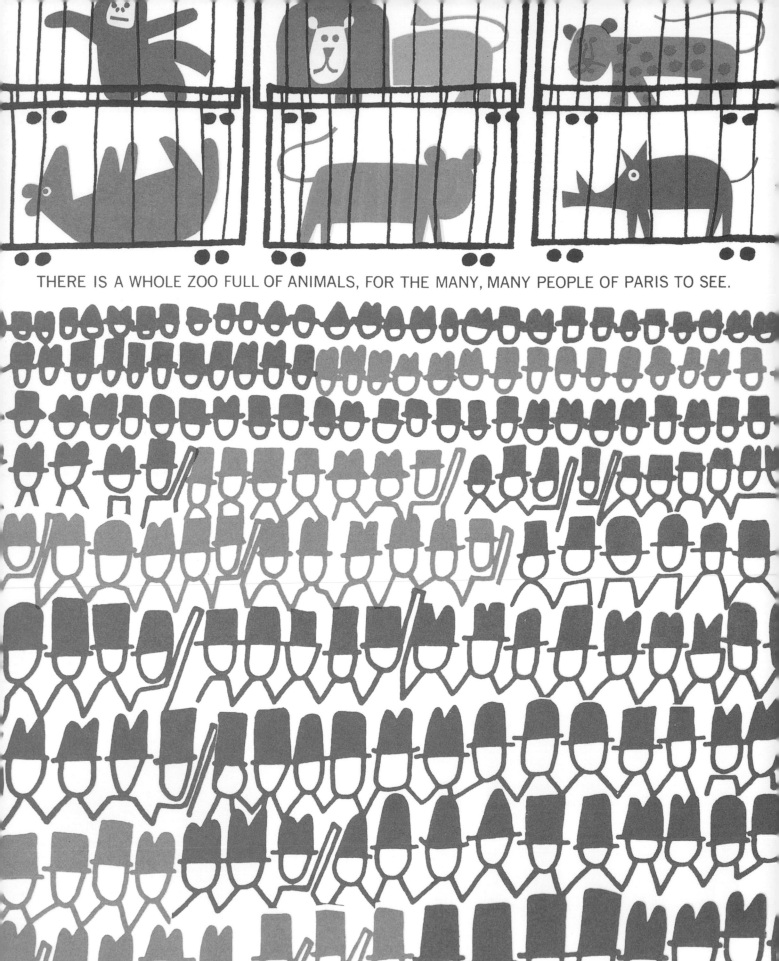

THERE IS A WHOLE ZOO FULL OF ANIMALS, FOR THE MANY, MANY PEOPLE OF PARIS TO SEE.

THERE ARE NOT MANY PEOPLE IN REBOUL.

THERE
IS
MONSIEUR
MANGER,
THE
BAKER.

THERE
IS
MONSIEUR
GOGI,
THE
MAILMAN.

THERE
IS
MADAME
CRÈME,
WHO
HAS
THE COW,

AND
GEORGES, WHO
DRIVES
THE
BUS

AND A FEW MORE.

OH, HOW HENRI WANTS TO SEE PARIS! ONE DAY, HE CANNOT WAIT ANY LONGER. SO, OFF HE GOES! HE TAKES SOME CHEESE, A CARROT, AND A PIECE OF BREAD IN A PAPER BAG. HENRI ALSO TAKES A PENCIL AND A PIECE OF PAPER WITH HIM. HE WILL MAKE PICTURES OF PARIS FOR HIS FRIENDS.

HENRI WALKS AND WALKS. HE SEES A COW EATING GRASS AND A BIRD EATING A

WORM.

AFTER A WHILE HENRI GETS TIRED. HE GETS HUNGRY TOO.

SO HENRI
STOPS TO
EAT HIS
OWN LUNCH.
"NOW I WILL
SLEEP,"
SAYS HENRI,
"BUT HOW
WILL I KNOW
WHICH WAY
TO GO
WHEN I
WAKE UP?"

"I KNOW,"
SAYS HENRI.
(HENRI IS
VERY SMART.)
AND HE
PUTS HIS
PENCIL DOWN
WITH
THE TIP
OF THE PENCIL
POINTING
ON THE ROAD
TO PARIS.

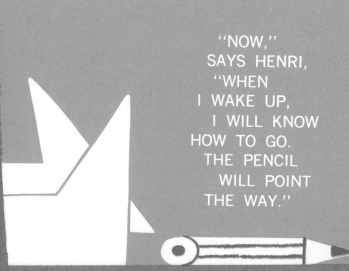

"NOW,"
SAYS HENRI,
"WHEN
I WAKE UP,
I WILL KNOW
HOW TO GO.
THE PENCIL
WILL POINT
THE WAY."

AND HENRI SLEEPS.

WHILE
HE
SLEEPS,
A LITTLE
BIRD
SEES THE
PENCIL
IN THE ROAD.

"THIS PENCIL IS JUST THE
RIGHT SIZE FOR MY NEST,"
SAYS THE SMALL BIRD.

AND
THE
LITTLE BIRD
TAKES
THE
PENCIL
OFF TO HIS
NEST.

BUT
THE BIRD
IS VERY
LITTLE. AND
THE NEST
IS LITTLE TOO.
THE PENCIL IS TOO
BIG FOR THE
LITTLE
BIRD'S
NEST.
SO—

THE
BIRD
DROPS
THE
PENCIL
BACK
ON
THE
ROAD—

JUST
ABOUT
WHERE
HENRI
HAD
PUT IT.
JUST
ABOUT!

AT LAST HENRI WAKES UP. IT IS GETTING LATE. HE MUST HURRY
TO PARIS. BUT WHICH WAY IS PARIS? HENRI LOOKS AT THE PENCIL.

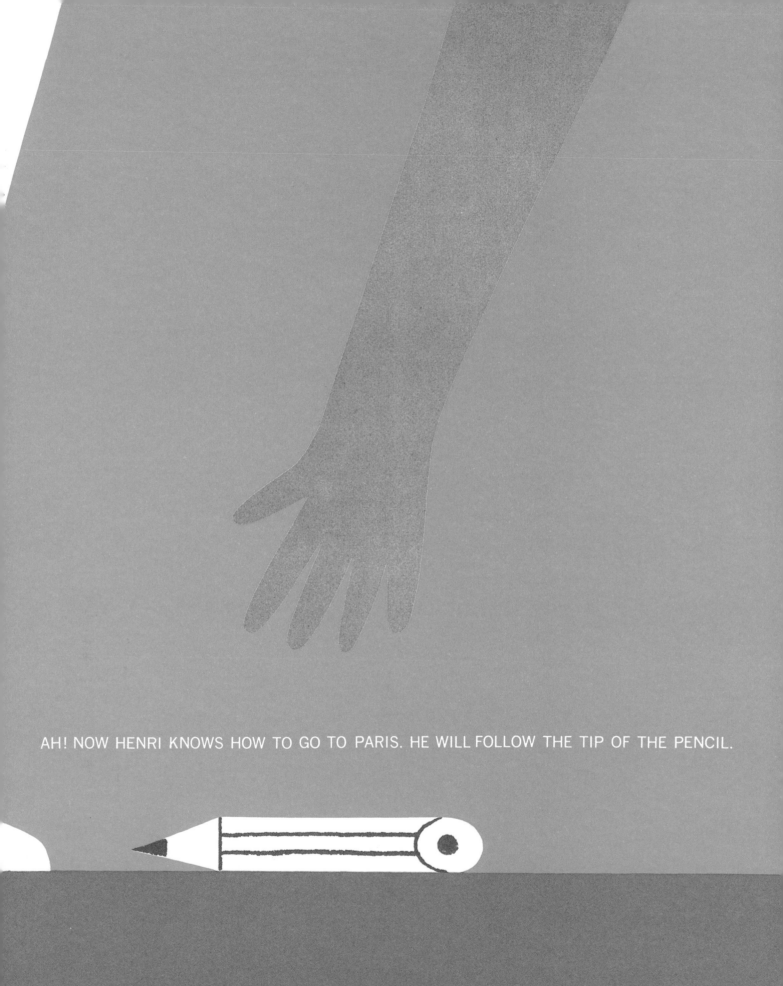

AH! NOW HENRI KNOWS HOW TO GO TO PARIS. HE WILL FOLLOW THE TIP OF THE PENCIL.

THE BIRD WATCHES HENRI. HENRI WALKS AND WALKS.

SOON HE SEES
A CITY.
"AH," SAYS HENRI.
"PARIS!"
"LIKE REBOUL,"
SAYS HENRI.
HENRI GOES INTO THE
CITY. HE SEES A PARK.
IN THE PARK ARE
FIVE TREES,
ONE SQUIRREL, AND
A SMALL GRAY CHURCH.
"WHAT A PRETTY PARK,"
SAYS HENRI.
"IT IS JUST LIKE THE
PARK WE HAVE IN REBOUL."

A BUS STOPS AT THE PARK. IT IS THE ONLY BUS IN SIGHT. WHO GETS OFF THE BUS? WHY —

MONSIEUR
MANGER,
THE
BAKER.

MONSIEUR
GOGI,
THE
MAILMAN.

MADAME
CRÈME,
WHO
HAS
THE COW,

AND
A FEW
OTHERS.

"EVERYONE
IS IN
PARIS
TODAY"
SAYS HENRI.
"JUST
LIKE
ME."

HENRI SEES
A STREET.
IT IS A STREET
JUST LIKE
HIS STREET IN
REBOUL.
HENRI WALKS DOWN
THE STREET.
THERE, AT THE END
OF THE STREET,
IS A NICE HOUSE.
IT IS LITTLE
AND WHITE.

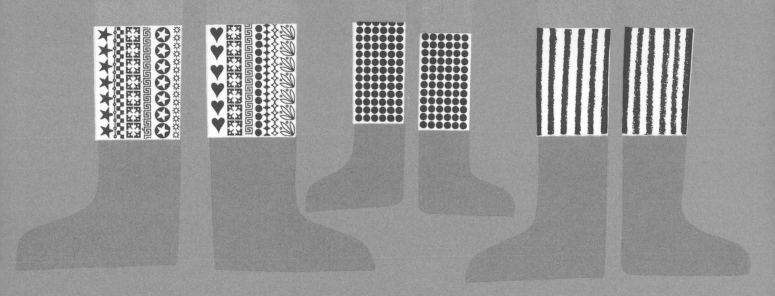

THREE BOYS ARE PLAYING OUTSIDE THE HOUSE. WHAT ARE THEIR NAMES?
WHY ANDRÉ, JACQUES, AND MICHEL! THEY ARE HENRI'S THREE FRIENDS!

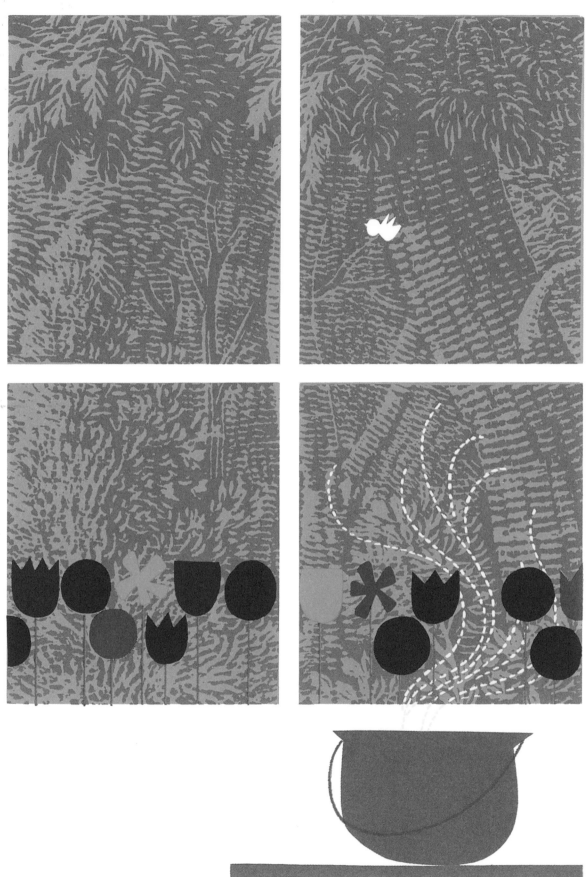

HENRI OPENS THE DOOR OF THE HOUSE AND GOES IN. THERE ARE FLOWERS AT THE WINDOW. THERE IS GOOD SOUP ON THE STOVE.

HENRI'S MOTHER AND FATHER ARE INSIDE THE HOUSE TOO. THEY SMILE AT HENRI.

"OH, MOTHER,"
SAYS HENRI.
"HELLO FATHER,"
SAYS HENRI.
"IT IS NICE
TO SEE YOU AGAIN.
BUT DO YOU KNOW
SOMETHING? I AM
JUST AS
MUCH AT HOME
IN PARIS AS I AM IN
REBOUL."

WHAT DO
YOU
THINK
OF THAT?

ME